Emily Gravett

BEAR & HARE

Go Fishing

Simon & Schuster Books for Young Readers
New York   London   Toronto   Sydney   New Delhi

Bear and Hare are going fishing.

Bear LOVES fishing!

Bear fished. He fished . . .

Hare's hat.

He fished . . .

a frog!

He fished . . .

a roller skate.

Bear fished.

He fished . . .

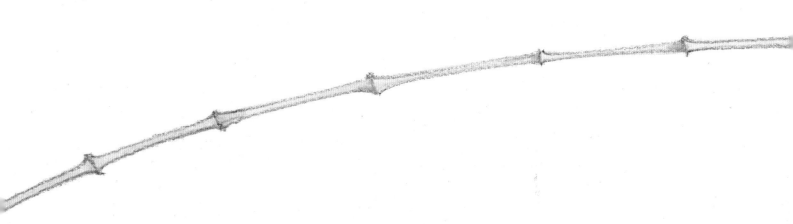

and fished . . .

and . . .

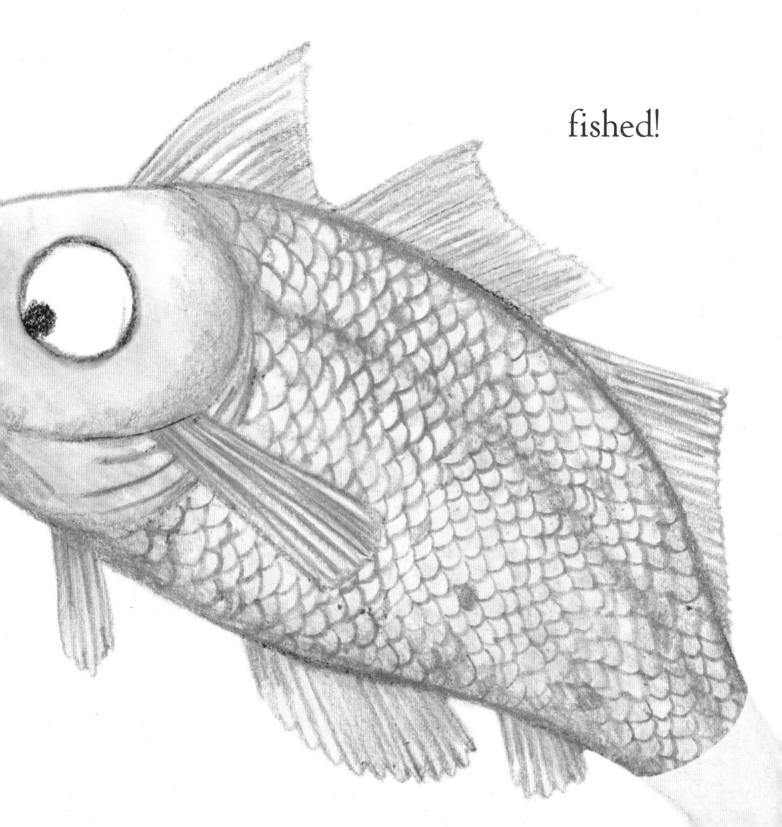

fished!

For Cecily & Laily

SIMON & SCHUSTER BOOKS FOR YOUNG READERS • An imprint of Simon & Schuster Children's Publishing Division • 1230 Avenue of the Americas, New York, New York 10020 • Copyright © 2014 by Emily Gravett • Originally published in 2014 in Great Britain by Macmillan Children's Books. Published by arrangement with Macmillan Publishers Limited. • First US edition 2015 • All rights reserved, including the right of reproduction in whole or in part in any form. • SIMON & SCHUSTER BOOKS FOR YOUNG READERS is a trademark of Simon & Schuster, Inc. • For information about special discounts for bulk purchases, please contact Simon & Schuster Special Sales at 1-866-506-1949 or business@simonandschuster.com. • The Simon & Schuster Speakers Bureau can bring authors to your live event. For more information or to book an event, contact the Simon & Schuster Speakers Bureau at 1-866-248-3049 or visit our website at www.simonspeakers.com. • The text for this book is set in Baskerville. • The illustrations for this book are rendered in pencil, watercolor, and wax crayons. • Manufactured in China • 1014 MCM • 10 9 8 7 6 5 4 3 2 1 • CIP data for this book is available from the Library of Congress • ISBN 978-1-4814-2289-5 • ISBN 978-1-4814-2290-1 (eBook)